This Topsy and Tim book belongs to

_____

Topsy and Tim
Start School

By Jean and Gareth Adamson

Illustrations by Belinda Worsley

A catalogue record for this book is available from the British Library

Published by Ladybird Books Ltd
A Penguin Company
Penguin Books Ltd., 80 Strand, London WC2R 0RL, UK
Penguin Books Australia Ltd., 707 Collins Street, Melbourne, Victoria 3008, Australia
Penguin Group (NZ) 67 Apollo Drive, Rosedale, North Shore 0632, New Zealand

019

© Jean and Gareth Adamson MCMXCV
Reissued MMXIV

ISBN: 978-1-40930-083-0
Printed in China

www.topsyandtim.com

Topsy and Tim were off to school after a fantastic summer holiday. They felt happy and excited. They walked straight past their old nursery.

Topsy and Tim were going to join the bigger children at the Primary School. They knew the Primary School was a cheerful, friendly place. They had been there already, on a visit. But Topsy and Tim held hands as they went through the big gateway.

"Oh, look," said Tim.
"There's Tony Welch."
"Hi, Tony!" called Topsy,
but her voice came out not
quite loud enough.

The Primary School was much noisier than their old nursery. Some of the bigger children did look very big. Topsy and Tim soon met several of their old friends, as well as Tony.

Miss Terry was
Topsy and Tim's
class teacher.

She showed them where to hang their coats and bags.
Each peg had a different picture by it.
"Remember your special picture," said Miss Terry,
"and then you will know your own peg."

"My peg's got a rabbit like Wiggles," said Topsy.
Tim's peg had a picture of a black umbrella.

He wasn't sure he could remember an old umbrella.
"Girls always get the best things," grumbled Tim.

Mummy took Topsy and Tim into their new classroom.

"There's Tony again," said Topsy. They went to see what he was doing.

Tony was busy doing a jigsaw puzzle.
"Would you like to do a jigsaw puzzle,
Topsy and Tim?" said Miss Terry.

Topsy and Tim found plenty of interesting things to do. There was sand to dig in and water for sailing and sploshing. The home corner had scales that worked.

When they felt like looking at books
and pictures, they sat on the carpet in
the quiet corner. The bell for playtime
seemed to ring too soon.

Miss Terry led the children into the school playground. It was full of big boys and girls all making a noise.

Topsy and Tim stayed close to
Miss Terry for a while.

Soon Topsy and Tim were
playing happily with some new
friends. Then a big boy rang a
loud bell. Everybody stopped
playing and stood in lines to go
back into school.

Dinner was served by two
jolly ladies, Miss Knitting
and Mrs Pie. At least,
Topsy and Tim thought
those were their names.
Topsy was astonished to
see Tim eat all his greens.

Afternoon school was more like their old nursery. Miss Terry gathered all the children round her. They sang some clever songs, with actions.

When it was time to go home, Topsy and Tim went
to put on their jackets.
"I can remember my peg picture," said Tim proudly.
"It's an umbrella."
But Tim's peg was empty. Tim was upset.

"Never mind, Tim," said Miss Terry. "This often
happens. I expect someone knocked your things
down and put them back on the
wrong peg by mistake."

"Here's your jacket,"
called Andy Anderson.

"Did you enjoy your first day at big school?" asked Mummy on the way home. "Of course we did!" said Topsy and Tim.

*Now turn the page and help
Topsy and Tim solve a puzzle.*

All the children have their own peg for their coats and bags. Read the clues. Can you work out which peg belongs to which child?

Topsy's peg has a picture of something white and fluffy.

Tim's peg has a picture of something that is useful in the rain.

The picture on Stevie's peg is of something fast and red.

The picture on Vinda's peg is of something you can live in.

Tony's peg has a picture of something that floats on water.

Kerry's peg has a picture of something pretty and pink.

A Map of
the Village

farm

Topsy and
Tim's house

Kerry's
house

Tony's
house

park

garage

health centre

post office

church

primary school

nursery school

police station

Have you read all the Topsy and Tim stories?

At the Farm — 9781409303367	**Go Camping** — 9781409303336	**Go on an Aeroplane** — 9781409300571
Go on a Train — 9781409304241	**Go to Hospital** — 9781409304234	
Start School — ✓ 9781409300830	**Go to the Doctor** — 9781409303343	**Go to the Dentist** — 9781409300588
Have a Birthday Party — 9781409300618	**Meet Father Christmas** — 9781409311591	
Meet the Police — 9781409308836	**Go to the Zoo** — 9781409300847	**Meet the Firefighters** — 9781409307211
Learn to Swim — 9781409300601	**Play Football** — 9781409303350	
Safety First — 9781409308829	**Sports Day** — 9781409309468	**Have Itchy Heads** — 9781409307204
The New Baby — 9781409300564	**Visit London** — 9781409309475	

All titles by Jean and Gareth Adamson.

The Topsy and Tim app is available for iPad,
iPhone and iPod touch.

It is also available on Android devices.